Who Created the Universe
&
Why?

"When science and spiritual depth travel together,
the distance to the destination is shortened."

Mahdy Khaiyat
From "A Cornucopia of Aphorisms"

*

"Science does not know its debt to
the imagination."

Ralph Waldo Emerson

*

"The universe is made of stories, not of atoms."

Poet Muriel Rukeyser

*

This is one of them.

Who Created the Universe & Why?

A story,
A provocative and entertaining narrative
attempting
to unlock
the mystery of creation.

*

Ibrahim Ibn Salma

Ask Publishing
Santa Barbara, California
USA

ISBN: 978-0-9850376-2-8

First Edition
10 9 8 7 6 5 4 3 2 1

Cover & Book Design by Cesar Stanley Hernandez
Book Production by ASK Publishing

Photograph by Ana Ruth Flores

Published by ASK Publishing
1061 N. Patterson Ave
Santa Barbara, CA   93111
805-252-1207
askpublishing1@gmail.com

Other books by the author:

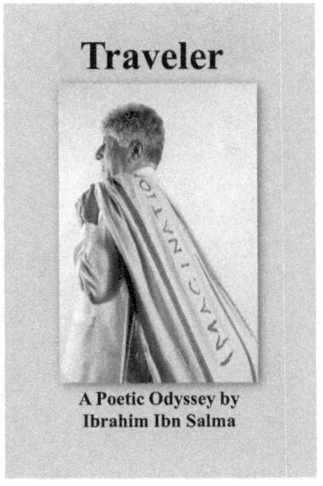

Traveler: a collection of poems,   2012

A poetic odyssey, exploring the meaning of our
spiritual nature. Through love and compassion
we may gain more understanding of ourselves
and the world around us. And, in the process, we
may solidify our genuine and honest connection
with family members, nature, our outer and inner
worlds and the Divine. It is a journey of learning
and discovery.

"Ibrahim escorts us on the path of spirit."

Dr. Spencer Sherman, PhD
Psychologist and Poet

House of Love: a collection of poems, 2013

The poems of this collection are stepping stones.
We step upon them to lead us to the House of Love.
In the House of Love, love becomes our sole moti-
vator. Once we enter, we shall never want to leave.

*"The brutality of the world is taught in these pages
how to move through mindfulness toward peace
by ingenious verbal strategies that capture the complexity and ultimate healing simplicity of the power
of love."*

*Barry Spacks, Poet-Professor, The First Poet
laureate of the city of Santa Barbara, California*

This book is dedicated
to
the soul of humanity.

Table of Contents

Description

"Who Created the Universe & Why?" is a spiritual parable with a poetic flavor. The essence is to demonstrate that spirituality and science can complement each other to shed some light upon who created this vast organized universe and why. It in no way claims the authenticity of the logic it explains. It floats with the art of storyteller to reach its findings without posing any challenges to religious beliefs or scientific theories. It has the courage to create a new way of thinking of what may have happened before the big bang which led to the manifestation of this wondrous universe.

"When the objectivity of reality meets
The subjectivity of consciousness,
We may begin to unlock
The mystery of creation."

Ibrahim Ibn Salma

Enjoy the story.

Characters

The father: Shaidan
The mother: Faribah
The seeker: Cidar, *(Ceedaar)*
The wife: Hishmat
The friend: Safeer
The consciousness Avatar: Waaii
The set theory Avatar: Jamii
The cell theory Avatar: Khalia
The energy Avatar: Tagha
The deity Avatar: Sama
The universe Avatar: Konna
The higher self Avatar: Aalii

Prelude

The objective of this story, despite its being fiction, is neither to promote scientific discoveries nor to interpret religion in a new way, but rather to assimilate realities by observing how the world and its physical laws work. The simplification of such laws and their applications may enhance human welfare and help transform the truths of science and religion into the structure of a broader and more purified spirituality which someday may stimulate intelligent effort to improve human conditions and the advancement in strength and excellence of character. It may also help create a more compassionate, loving, and harmonious world, devoid of racism and greed so that mankind may attain its highest possible welfare and happiness upon this earth.

The reader will find the ideas and the logical sequences raised in this book are similar in nature whether their source is physical or spiritual. A physical idea can also be applied with the same fashion in the spiritual world. A truth may not be the beginning, the middle, or the end. A truth might be the whole.

The thoughts which state that the universe is simply an accident that just happened versus the thought that a kind of intelligence beyond its boundaries responsible for its creation may both be logically applied and ostensibly complimentary to one another, meaning that science and religion (spirituality) may have collaborated to create this incredible vastness with its enormous complexity and precision. But this idea can only be true if the creator and the created are one and the same. Meaning that the creator passes the creative energy to the created and the created becomes a creator..

Let us not worry how the universe was created, but rather let us ask the questions: "Who created it" and "Why?"

The "Who" part of the question would initially be easy to address. We would think of it and without any hesitation we answer, "God created the universe". However, when we ask why God created the universe, we start stumbling over the answer. In his book "The Cosmic Game", Stan Graf attempts to answer the question by suggesting that God was bored, lonely, and maybe curious, wanting to do something or perhaps wishing to be worshiped and exalted. It seems to a normally intelligent mind that the answer to the "why" does not make sense. By this answer, Stan Graf has actually degraded the concept of God with these human-like qualities:

boredom, loneliness, curiosity, exaltation, and the desire to have something to do. Then we have to go back and reexamine the "who" and try to find an alternative answer so that the "why" would make sense and resonate with the "who". This story attempts to do just that. Enjoy.

Ibrahim Ibn Salma
Santa Barbara, 2014

1- The Farm

"To survive is to be most loving."
                              Ibrahim Ibn Salma

The door squeaked as it opened. Shaidan walked in, carrying a grocery bag. Cidar ran toward his father with joy and excitement, saying "Papa, Papa what's in the bag?"

"Lakaa," the father replied. (Lakaa means goodies.)

As he was about to sit on the couch, he mumbled, "Come and sit next to me." Cidar was happy to comply. Instead of sitting next to him, Cidar was clinging to his dad's legs as they straddled, curious to know what was in the bag. Shaidan, as usual, opened the bag slowly. With a radiant look in his eyes he took out a bunch of grapes and laid it on his lap. He picked one grape from the bunch, held a small knife he normally carried in his pocket and cut the grape into two halves. He gave one-half to Cidar and said as he was holding the other half in his hand, "Look how beautiful and sweet this grape is. Before you eat it, thank it for sacrificing its existence for us." His face became even more radiant as he put the half grape into his mouth and said, "Thank you grape." Cidar did the same.

Shaidan was in his forties, with a muscular build. He had been a farmer all his youthful life. He worked close to nature and what it provides. He was always appreciative and grateful for the good life he provided for his family. He would have been a Kabala if he were a Jew, a Sufi if he were a Muslim, or a St. Francis of Assisi if he were a Christian:

> The Sufi in you shines,
> When your mouth touches
> Every orb of vines.

But he was none of those. If you asked him who and what he is, he would recite the following poem:

> A voice called my name in a crowd,
> I turned around and looked.
>
> Who are you and
> Where do you come from?
>
> I will tell who I am,
> But I must first mention who I am not:
>
> I am not a Muslim, nor a Christian, nor a Jew,
> I am not a Buddhist, nor a Hindu, nor a Sufi,
>
> I have no guru or a leader to follow.
>
> My God dispenses neither rewards nor inflicts punishments,
> And promises neither Heaven nor Hell.

I am neither from the West nor the East,
Nor from any culture in between.

My Place is not a particular place,
And my dwelling is mother earth.

My nationality has no nation,
Nor a government to rule.

I look inside me
To attain the knowledge I seek,

I am just a human being
With a passion to feel.

Even though he was born and raised in Khamish-land and never traveled or experienced any other places, Shaidan looked at himself as a citizen of the world. He understood by being a farmer and working with soil and plants that all living things are somehow interconnected and that for life to continue there must be a co-operation and sacrifices among living organisms.

Cell Speaks

(On behalf of all cells)

In singles or groups we
Always existed.
You made us,
So that
We make you.

Fifty trillions of us
Live inside you in communion.
We survive because
We love one another;
The strong empower the weak -
All is powerful.
The healthy heal the sick -
All is healthy.
Yet,
We are commanded by
Your thoughts, feelings and emotions.
So,
Send us love -
Send us kindness -
Send us compassion;
We -
Send you life.

Faribah, on the other hand, was more practical and pragmatic as wife and mother. She took her household duties very seriously and prepared healthful and delicious meals for her husband Shaidan and their only son Cidar. She kept the house very clean, helped Cidar with his schooling and homework, and was always watching over the boy. She gave him a bath every night before bed, made sure he wore clean clothes and gently reminded him to behave while playing with other kids.

Cidar was not an ordinary child. He was acutely curious, wanted to know how and why things are the way they are. His head was full of questions and wondered about things that even older children did not seem to be curious about. He once asked his mother before bedtime, "Mommy, how did I come to this world?"

Faribah was very surprised by the question, and she was even more surprised by the fact that such a young child would ask such a question. However, she tried to soften her surprise and calmly she answered, "God put you in my stomach and I in turn delivered you to the world."

Cidar followed with another question, "Who is this God that put me in your stomach?"

"Oh, he is an old man with a white beard sitting up high in the sky, watching all of us and what we do. If we behave morally, he will guide us to heaven and if we behave immorally, he will put us in hell," Faribah responded.

"Why would he do that?" Cidar asked.

"I do not know, son," the mother fretfully answered and continued, "Now, stop asking any more questions, go to the bathroom and do potty, and then go to bed to sleep."

Cidar obeyed without any more questions. As he was pulling his pajamas down to urinate, he looked up and said, "God, are you watching me? You are watching me, aren't you?" He was frightened. He pulled up his pajamas, and ran out of the bathroom. His mother asked him if he did his business.

Cidar responded with tears in his eyes, "No, I could not because God was watching me." Faribah felt sad and remorseful as she held Cidar in her arms and said, "I am very sorry son; I forgot to tell you that God does not go to the bathroom." She continued as she carried him on her shoulder, "Come with me to the bathroom." She comforted him while he was trying to urinate. It took Cidar at least five minutes to quiet himself down and ultimately urinate. Faribah's compassionate response helped a little, but not much. Cidar, later in his life, continued taking a long time to urinate.

Despite some of these incidents, Cidar grew up in very caring and loving surroundings, sheltered by both of his parents' affection and compassion. However, at an early age, he developed his own character traits of stubbornness and willfulness, which at times caused some anxiety and discomfort.

When he was 6 years old, a classmate at school told him that medical doctors always wear glasses. Cidar took that thought as a matter of fact. A year later, he was sick with a fever and so weak that he could not leave the house to see a doctor. His dad asked the family doctor to come to the house to diagnose his son. Cidar would not allow the doctor to touch or even come near him. He was scream-ing and shouting "Don't come near me; you are not a doctor!!" His dad was baffled as to why his son thought the doctor was not a doctor. After a min-ute or so of a loud verbal exchange between Cidar and his dad about whether the doctor is a doctor or not a doctor, the doctor asked Cidar, "Cidar, why do you think I am not a doctor?"

Cidar started to catch his breath, cleared the tears from his eyes and responded with a sob, "Because you don't wear glasses, and doctors must wear glasses to be a doctor."

The doctor and Shaidan were surprised and amused at the same time. Without hesitation, the doctor reached into his briefcase, held up a pair of glasses, put them on and said to Cidar, "Now I am a doctor, I wear glasses."

Cidar looked with a smile of relief at the doctor and said, "Now you may touch me."

Shaidan was agitated and wanted to correct his son's false impression about doctors; but the doc-tor placed his hand on Shaidan's shoulder and in a calm voice said to him, "Let me talk to your son."

He turned to Cidar and with a soft voice said, "Open your mouth. I want to check your temperature." He continued as he was putting the thermometer in Cidar's mouth, "Doctors do not have to wear glasses unless they need them, like everybody else. I sometimes need to wear my glasses when I read. You may, when you grow older, need to wear glasses so that you can see well. Your temperature is not as high as I thought. You have a light fever and you will be OK, but you have to rest for a few days, drink a lot of liquid, and eat only soups. Do you have any questions?"

Cidar felt good and with a smile said, "Thank you, Doctor. Now I know you do not have to wear glasses." The doctor smiled back as he was leaving the bedroom. Shaidan was also pleased as he followed the doctor to the front door.

2- Tragedy

*"Our wounds are often the openings into the best and the
most beautiful part of us."*
                              David Richo

Years passed by, Cidar grew to be a fine, strong
man. After his father's passing, he inherited the
farm and worked hard to expand its business. He
married Hishmat, the sweetheart of his teen years.
She became his darling wife and the mother of his
two fine children.

He had everything a man could ever wish for: a
home, a successful business, a beautiful and responsible wife, and two lovely children. His mother
Faribah was also living with him. She had added
a loving and compassionate dimension to his life
with her wisdom and life-long experience. She was
about fifty years old, in excellent health, and was
able to help with small tasks around the farm. His
children had also benefited a great deal from her
love and affection. Cidar had much to be grateful
for.

For several years, the winter rain on Khamishland
was below normal, which caused an increasing
possibility of a severe drought. Even though Cidar
prepared for such a possibility, his crops and cattle
always needed plenty of water during springs and

summers. His crop output gradually diminished, and he was not able to generate enough business. One year he had to apply for more water from the neighboring lands. Despite the fact that his application was accepted, the amount of water he was getting was not enough to last the whole summer. He was not able to sleep the night before the day he was supposed to go and claim the allotted water, thinking all night about what he had to do to save his crops and cattle with insufficient water. His wife Hishmat prepared a good breakfast with plenty of coffee to help him stay awake before he left for his trip. His water truck was only able to hold three thousand gallons of water on each trip, which meant he had to make ten trips to get the thirty thousand gallons reserved for him.

During his sixth trip he was exhausted. He had to let his employees go because he could not pay them and consequently he did not have anybody helping him drive the truck. As he was trying to stay awake while driving, another truck from the opposite direction was approaching very fast in the same lane. Cidar could not avoid the head-on collision. He was thrown out of the truck, several feet in the air. As he was falling down back to the ground, he felt he was being kept in the air by a mysterious power, with a slow descent to the ground almost like an airplane landing. He closed his eyes as he was approaching the ground. He hardly felt the impact.

With neither pain nor broken limbs, he was able to stand and walk on his feet. He spotted his truck in the distance. It was badly damaged. He walked to the other damaged truck to check on the driver, who was lying in a pool of blood, unconscious. Cidar felt his pulse, and detected no sign of life. The man was dead.

Cidar was shocked and overwhelmed by what had just happened to him. He suddenly had a fatal accident. His water truck had collided head on with another truck. The two trucks were badly damaged. He was miraculously spared from injury and perhaps a sure death. The other truck driver did not escape death. Why? Why? He repeatedly asked himself. Why did he land softly on the ground?, What or who carried him and defied the force of gravity to save him from being injured or killed? While these thoughts were swirling in his head, he heard a siren approaching from a distance. A fire truck and an ambulance arrived at the accident scene. The medical team found him completely unharmed while they pronounced the other driver dead.

"How did you escape injury?" one fireman asked Cidar.

"I am wondering myself," Cidar replied.

"Thank God for your safety" the fireman murmured and asked Cidar, "Do you need a ride any-
where?"

"Yes, to my farm ten miles down the road," Cidar
replied.

The fireman handed Cidar a piece of paper and
said, "This is the report of the accident; it may help
with your insurance claim."

"Thanks," Cidar said.

As the fire truck approached Cidar's farm, a col-
umn of smoke was rising up from the direction of
the farm. Cidar's heart started beating faster. He
was wondering what was happening to the farm.
He said to the fireman driving the truck, "Where is
that smoke coming from? I hope my farm and my
family are safe. I would not like to have more bad
things happen to me."

The fireman replied, "It looks as though the smoke
is coming up from a big building or a cluster of
buildings. I will go faster." He sounded the siren
and made a radio call for more help.

As they got closer to the fire, it appeared that the
main house and the nearby barns of Cidar's farm
were all on fire. The flame was so huge and high

that there was not much left to salvage. Cidar was looking around to see if any members of his family were out and safe. He could see no one. As soon as the truck stopped, he rushed out and ran toward the house as it was being completely burned to the ground. He was screaming for his mother, his wife and his children.

The fireman ran up behind him, trying to stop him from going into the raging fire as he was looking for his family. The fireman was able to grab him and hold him as he got closer to what was left of the front door. No sound, movements, or screams for help were coming from the inside of the house except the sound of the burning fire.

The reinforcement of more firemen and more trucks had arrived. They started putting the fire out. Cidar was looking on with tears in his eyes, wondering what had come down upon him. What tragic events, one after another had dropped, all of a sudden, upon him? He may have lost the most precious thing in his life, his family. As he was lost in his grief, the fire captain came to him and told him of the inevitable and devastating news, "Sir, we have managed to put out the fire, and I am sorry to say that we could not save any members of your family; they are all dead. Would you please come in to identify their bodies?"

Cidar stood motionless and said nothing; he became pale and suddenly collapsed on the ground.
The fireman hurried to check on him and felt his
pulse as he was calling his crew for help. The pulse
was ok. The firemen carried Cidar to the ambulance and took him to a nearby hospital for a
checkup.

When Cidar regained consciousness a few hours
later, he initially did not know where he was. A
nurse approached his bed carrying a tray of food
and drinks. Cidar did not feel hungry, but the nurse
insisted that he must eat. He then realized that he
was being treated in a hospital. As he tried to put
some of the food in his mouth, he remembered
what had happened to him. He looked at the nurse
with watery eyes and said, "I lost the most precious
thing in my life, my family. I lost my wife, my two
children, and my dear mother; I lost them all. The
business could be easily replaced, but not my family. I can never replace my mother with her compassion and love."

The nurse sympathized with him and said, "I feel
so sorry for you. Try to think of what good could
come out from all of this."

Cidar wondered, "Yes, how I was spared from
death when my truck was completely destroyed.
Dying with the rest of my family would have been

much easier to bear. I have no clue as to why I am still alive."

"That is for you to discover," the nurse interrupted. "If I were you, I would dedicate the rest of my life to finding out. I think you still have some work to do before you leave this earth. You are destined to do something, I believe, and your destiny would not have been realized if you had your family and business … or … if you were dead. Think about it. Remember what Rumi said, " the nurse added, *(Where there is ruin, there is hope for a treasure.)* Cidar, rendered silent, could not utter a word. The nurse continued, "The doctor said you can leave any time." Then she left the room.

Cidar found some comfort in her words and felt that a new life was to be written for him. But what kind of life? And what kind of power had saved his life? He had more questions than answers.

3-The Destiny

"Our destiny is not written for us, it is written by us."

Barack Obama

Cidar was then 31 years old and alone for the first time. He may have been lonelier than he had ever been. It was as if something inside him had died. The loved ones he had known and the business he had mastered had all suddenly vanished. There was a metaphoric death occurring inside him as he tried to move beyond his struggles. One day while he was deep in thought, he remembered what his father once told him, "Some things and people in life sacrifice themselves for others to live on, like the grape we are about to eat."

Did his entire family know what he was destined to do, and by having them in his life he would not have even thought of doing? Did his farm, his cattle, and his crops realize Cidar's purpose in life? Did they have to disappear out of his life for him to fulfill it? So many unanswered questions filled his head. What the nurse had said to him before he left the hospital continued to reverberate in his mind, "If I were you, I would dedicate the rest of my life to finding out what it was." He recalled the comforting feeling he felt when he heard her say these words and then quoted Rumi. So many challenges confronted him. He felt as though he were besieged from every side.

As soon as he got out of the hospital, he worked on collecting the insurance compensation for his losses. This left him with a sizable fund to live on until his next move. He rented a small, modestly furnished studio in the quiet town of Khamish with modest pieces of furnishings. He began to adapt to being alone. It was, in the beginning, very difficult to do, but he felt he had to do it. He met new people and shaped some level of friendship with a few. He even found a part-time job as a dishwasher in a busy restaurant in town. He figured to have some income so that his savings would not be depleted. He started getting used to his new and challenging life, totally self-reliant -- learning how to cook and eat alone, how to clean and dust, and how to do his own laundry.

Despite being surrounded by all these repetitive and insignificant tasks, Cidar found ample time to think and contemplate. His desire to understand the power that saved his life had grown strong inside him. He began to go to the nearby Buddhist and Hindu temples to learn some of their spiritual practices and philosophies. He learned that people suffer because they get attached to other people and things around them, that they create Karma from everything they say and do. He started to learn how to relax alone and meditate, which he grew to enjoy more as he continued practicing. He found himself spending more time meditating than going to the temples. While meditating, he kept asking about the nature of the power that saved his life, but to no avail. He became frustrated and impatient, thinking he must be pursuing the wrong path. He then resumed frequenting the temples to look for answers.

Safeer was a down-to-earth fellow and frequent attendee at the Buddhist temple. He met Cidar there, and as they spent time together, their friendship grew strong. They strolled in the foothills of the nearby Mont Taba Mountain and talked about many different things.

One afternoon, after Cidar left work, he thought of calling Safeer and asking him to meet at Mont Taba. Safeer agreed and when they met, Safeer suggested hiking up the mountain. As they were hiking up, Safeer stopped for a moment and looked at Cidar and said, "Look at this rock, Cidar. I would like to say something to her."

Cidar instantly interrupted and surprisingly questioned him "How would you say something to an inanimate object, like a rock? Do you think she would be able to hear you and understand you?"

Safeer with a confident voice said, "Yes, I believe rocks, water, and trees are able to hear us and understand what we say. They even try to say something back to us. We are the ones who don't understand what they say."

"I have to think about what you just said, Safeer," Cidar followed. "OK, for now tell me what you were going to say to the rock."

"I would tell the rock," Safeer said. "Rock, support me when I step on you so that I won't fall. If I ever fall, which is my fault not yours, be a sponge for me so I will not break my bones. Tell the rocks every time you hike what you want them to do for you. They will listen. " Cidar was dumbfounded.

Hiker

Rocks to climb, creeks to cross,
Views to opine, trees to hug.

Hearts to pulsate,
Sweat to gush.

Mountain wanderers
Traverse the trails.

Rocks grow friendly,
Supportive of every footfall.

Sponges they become

With every sudden sprawl.

The sun sank behind the summit of Mont Taba and crimson clouds haloed the remaining sunrays. Cidar and Safeer had thought to return home before dark. As they were walking down the mountain, the trees and the rocks became blended in a somber mass, ready to fall asleep. Overhead the stars began to shine one by one as the darkness gradually enveloped the path they were traversing. When they approached Cidar's studio, they wished each other a good night's sleep as they parted.

Cidar became fond of Safeer and wanted to see him and talk with him more often. He felt he could share his deepest feelings with him, and grew more trusting of him. One day Cidar thought of telling Safeer about his frustration with not understanding the nature of the power that saved his life. He asked Safeer if he knew anything about such powers.

"I do not know anything about the nature of the power that saved your life, Cidar," Safeer responded. He continued, "It seems to me that that particular power is personal to you and came only to rescue you and no one else. I would suggest you continue searching for it inside yourself."

"How?" Cidar questioned.

"Meditation and more meditation," Safeer answered. "It is one of the best ways to explore your own inner world."

Truth

Truth-seeking from without
Is outlightenment.
Truth-seeking from within
Is enlightenment.

4- Mont Taba

"We sit together, the mountain and me, until only the mountain remains."
                                        Li Po

Cidar thought of what Safeer suggested and remembered the times when he actually enjoyed meditating. Though it did not give him any clues or answers to his question, he felt more at ease dealing with his surroundings and everyday life after each meditation. One day, when the sun was bright and the air was comfortably warm, he thought of taking a walk in the foothills of Mont Taba. As he walked and looked at the trees, rocks, and the wild flowers which were beginning to bloom with early spring, he felt a connection to nature. He remembered when Safeer and he were hiking together and when Safeer was talking to a rock. He began doing the same and talking to all of them, even though he was still skeptical of whether they heard him. They, however, reminded him of his farm. But it was more than a reminder. The feeling plunged deeper. He felt that nature was not there for him to commercially sell or buy. It was there to form a deeper connection which he did not understand at the moment. As he was looking at Mont Taba he noticed a thick cloud covering its highest peak. A quivering sensation filled his body and reminded him of his dear mother when she breast-fed him, perhaps he was two years old. Tears welled up his eyes.

Breast-fed

Mountaintops hug the clouds,
Rain drops on the mouth,
Milk filters through the blouse.

A tree in the distance caught his attention and brought him back to the present moment. He felt his feet were leading him to the tree, as if drawn by a magnet. Its branches seemed welcoming and comforting. As Cidar sat in the shade of the tree, a feeling of comfort and calmness suddenly fell upon him. He sensed his mother nearby looking over his shoulder. He continued looking at the mountain as the cloud parted on its peak. He briefly closed his eyes and thanked his mother for dropping by. A short time passed; he opened his eyes and looked at the surrounding fields, becoming intoxicated by nature and its beauty. He even thanked the tree for providing shade for him.

He held that feeling in his mind as he was walking back home. He sat down at home to rest and dozed off momentarily. The image of the tree whose shade he had sought appeared in front of his mind's eyes and spoke to him:

Tree Speaks

I
paint the sky
with my branches,
I fortify the soil with
my roots,   I fill the air
with oxygen, for a million
years I have given you the reason
and   the   resources   to exist,
my branches   never kill one another,
my roots never tell my fruits: "I owe you".
You have butchered, burned and demolished me,
and I have no desire to reciprocate, in lieu,
I have continued to give you more oxygen
and food and never retaliate, I wish
you would treat one another like
I have treated you for years.
Stop over and
give me
a hug sometimes.

Cidar opened his eyes right away and wrote down on a piece of paper what the tree had told him. He thought Safeer may have been right. Those inanimate objects truly hear us and even respond to us. He took a deep breath as he was leaving the studio, heading back to the tree. "I am so sorry. I apologize for all mankind for what we have put you through" Cidar said to the tree. He got closer and gave it a hug. Cidar was not the same person ever again. He increased his frequent visits to Mont Taba and the tree. He would give the tree a hug with every visit. He also sensed the presence of his mother nearby. He began to explore more of the mountain and felt an increasing connection with every rock on the hills and every stream flowing through them. A spiritual bond was formed with Mont Taba.

Mont Taba

A time we spent
Near your lower hills,

Your stones greeted us
And spoke to us of love.

Out of your rocks
We built a temple
To guard our union -
A child-like encounter
We never outgrew,

We played the game of innocence
On your chilled top.
Our embraced souls
Shrouded by your snowflakes,
Never shivered, never quivered,
Never wanted to part,

A game we thought we would
Never stop playing.

" *We began as a mineral,*
We emerged into plant life
And into animal state,
And then into being human,
And always we have forgotten
Our former state,
Except in early spring,
When we slightly recall
Being green again."

Rumi

Evolution of a Soul

Once I was a rock;
Against all odds, solid and firm I stood.

Then I was water;
Around obstacles I flowed to continue my journey.

When I was a tree; I stood tall and brushed the heavens
Yet my roots were deep into the earth.

When I was a bird; I learned
To fly and freely soar.

Now I am human; I am learning
How to love and be loved.

Cidar stopped analyzing what had happened
to him and started enjoying the experience. He
thought of doing his meditations under the tree
during the summer months, before fall and win-

ter arrived. The sun was shining most of the day and the weather was warm so he was able to reach deeper meditative states. He even sensed more energy from the tree and the mountain as he continued hugging and talking to them. He felt at home and deeply connected with his surroundings.

5- The Consciousness Avatar: Waaii

"I believe that my greatest labor should be devoted to seeking a beautiful simplicity."
                                        Christoph Gluck

Cidar kept returning to meditate under the tree despite his increased responsibilities at work. He was promoted to assistant cook for breakfast and lunch. He was never distracted, dedicating his time between three and five o'clock in the afternoon to relaxation, contemplation, and meditation under the tree. He grew fond of talking more to the rocks, the trees, and the brooks of mountain Taba. He sensed them as his newly-found friends.

One evening upon his return from his meditation session at Mont Taba, Cidar fixed himself a light supper of salad made of fresh vegetables he bought from the farmers' market. The meal reminded him of foods he used to eat with his family in his farm. His eyes dropped a tear or two.

Before he got ready to go to bed, he would normally take a shower, as his mother brought him up to do. As he was ready to get into the shower, he noticed a small spider on the left side wall of the shower. He was about to turn the shower on, when something made him stop. He thought if he ran the shower the spider would drown and die. If he was able to talk to inanimate objects, he could probably talk to insects.

He said to the spider, "Hi spider, you are invading my space. This is my shower. If I turn on the shower, you would drown and die. I will give you five minutes to leave my shower." Cidar came back to the shower five minutes later. The spider, however, had not moved a leg. Cidar continued the dialog, "Well, it seems you don't care if you die. I will tell you what; I will not kill you. I will save your life." He held a piece of a toilet paper and let it hang near the spider. The spider leg-gripped the paper with enthusiasm. Cidar carried her out of the shower and let her drop on the bathroom floor. After his shower and as he was ready to go sleep, he noticed the same spider in the upper right corner of his studio. Cidar said with a soft voice talking to the spider, "I just saved your life; what are you doing here and what else do you want from me?" Naturally, the spider said nothing, or perhaps she said something and Cidar did not understand it then.

In the morning, after a restful night of sleep, Cidar woke up and noticed the spider was gone with no trace of a cobweb. Cidar, after few moment of thinking, realized what the spider was trying to tell him, "You saved my life, I will not leave messy cobwebs in your place. Thank you." Cidar was thrilled to make a new friend.

Spider

Visiting the tub of a mighty giant,
Prior to a warm bath of bubbly delight,

Not realizing the coming of a mortal plight,

With a newspaper neatly folded
His earthly existence slightly extended,

A second visit to the upper corner
Of the bedroom sighted, as the day
Folded its wings and parted,

A depth of gratitude for a life saved,
Telepathically communicated,
Followed by a peaceful dreamy sight,

As the sun heaved its rays
No web left behind.

For a few weeks, into early summer, Cidar's meditations got deeper and longer as the days progressed. He found himself more and more in tune with his own inner world. The longer he meditated, the deeper the awareness he reached. One day in early summer he was in a deep meditative state, when a human-like figure appeared to his inner sight and spoke; "Hello Cidar." Cidar became afraid of what and who the figure could be.

"Relax, do not be afraid. I am here to help you and work with you."

"Who are you?" Cidar cried out.

"My name is Waaii and I am a part, among other parts, of your higher self. I came to your awareness because you called us."

"I never called you," Cidar interrupted.

"Yes you did," Waaii responded, "when you were wondering about the nature of the power that saved your life. And here you are, doing all these meditations to find an answer. And here I am trying to tell you what you have been asking all along. The rest of your higher self is going to reveal even more and explain to you the real purpose behind saving your life and extending your lifetime on this earth."

"What is my higher self?" Cidar wondered.

"In due time, I will explain to you the nature of your higher self. For now, I would like to give you a faster and more reliable technique to reach the awareness of your higher self so that we can easily communicate with your conscious mind.
Waaii continued, "When you relax to meditate, imagine yourself going into the earth. Descend on a long stairway deeper into the earth. Try to feel the

earth and the soil, and smell the deep earth. At the
bottom of the stairway you will find a gate. Look
for the gatekeeper, an old man with a white beard
shrouded with a long white robe. Greet him with
a bow. With humility ask him to open the gate.
When he opens the gate, he will ask you to enter.
Thank him and walk through the gate. You will find
yourself in the middle of a rose garden. There will
be two empty chairs near the water fountain. Sit on
one of them and wait. One of us will appear to talk
with you."

The figure promptly disappeared from Cidar's view.
When Cidar came out of the meditation he sighed
and took a deep breath as he tried to collect his
thoughts. He looked at the time and noticed that
the meditation took only ten minutes. So many
things took place in a very short time; it was as
if time were irrelevant. More importantly, he felt
comfortable with the message Waaii spoke to him.
Despite a slight skepticism, he wanted to believe
what he had heard. Before he retired to his bed that
night, he wrote down the meditation instructions
Waaii had given him.

The following day – after work, Cidar walked towards Mont Taba and sat under the tree. He closed
his eyes and started to relax. He followed Waaii's
instructions. He sensed how welcoming the gatekeeper was. After he thanked him for opening the

gate, Cidar entered the garden and looked with an awe and amazement at a most beautiful garden, inducing a state of peace and serenity. Beds of colorful roses traced patches of red, white, and yellow along the edges of the garden.

Ode to Roses

Beauty of all beauties,
The universe, to the furthest stars
Illuminated by your infinite peace,

Romance begins when your rose-bed blooms
As you are gifted to lovers.

The reds are kissed by
The scarlet lips of the compassionates;

The glow of the full moon envies
Your whites;

Your yellows grieve for
Being separated from the beloved.

Yet,

Your colorful existence remains the bond

For love.

A fountain in the center was made of ancient stones, resembling the ones he saw of Mont Taba. A light scent of rose blossoms drifted to Cidar, capturing his attention. In the midst of his amazement he noticed two chairs by the fountain, exactly as Waaii had described. He sat down on one of them and waited. Waaii then appeared on the other chair. After he greeted Cidar, he asked, "How do you like the rose garden?"

"I love it; to me it reflects a monumental gateway to a blossoming world," Cidar responded and continued, "I feel that the whole garden seems to move and dance to the music of the Pastoral Symphony."

"I want you to be peaceful and comfortable with your surroundings," Waaii said as he sensed some doubtful look on Cidar's face.

"I would be if I could get rid of my skepticism that whatever is happening to me is real, and you are actually what you say you are," Cidar responded.

"I sensed you have some doubt. I can only say to you for now, Cidar, that the longer we meet and talk, the less doubtful and more trusting you will become. I suggest to you at this moment to allow the process and the experience to unfold," Waaii said.

"Yes, please continue." Cidar said.

"Great, now we can begin." Waaii continued. "You asked me about your higher self. Before I begin, I want you to know that whatever knowledge you receive in this garden may be of a great value, not just to you, but to others, both women and men. It is your choice, Cidar, to do whatever you please with it."

"I understand," Cidar responded.

Waaii continued, "Now let us talk about higher consciousness. What is its definition? Rather, what is the definition of consciousness? In order to answer this question you need to go beyond your limited physical thinking, past your five senses. With simplicity, I could answer,

"Consciousness is awareness. The more aware a person is the more conscious she or he is. Since you do exist in a physical world, you are limited by time, space, and using your five senses as you increase your awareness. In a particular time and place by employing your senses, you become aware of what is happening around you. You, therefore, are conscious of events and objects that your senses are capable of hearing, touching, smelling, tasting, and seeing. And for the things which you cannot see, hear, touch, smell, and taste but somehow you know to exist, you use your thoughts, feelings, and beliefs to become aware of their existence. So you have to leap beyond your physical senses to fully understand consciousness. I divide consciousness into four levels: personal conscious, personal unconscious, or subconscious, collective unconscious, and the higher conscious.

"I would define the four levels of consciousness as follows:

"The personal conscious level:
It is unique to you, containing the reality of your senses, thoughts, feelings and beliefs. It is your total awareness, the awareness of who you are and what you are. The level of its power varies with the levels of its awareness.

"The subconscious level:
It is unique and personal also. It is where your conscious mind stores your past realities and experiences, which in turn may or may not influence your present lifetime. Therefore, your past senses, thoughts, feelings, and beliefs, with their experiences, are all stored in the subconscious level.

For example, if you try to recall what you had for dinner on the 22nd of March 1999, you may find it impossible to recall such detail. But the subconscious level of your mind knows the answer because when the event took place, your conscious mind stored its content in your subconscious mind and it will stay there forever. Knowing how to access information stored in your subconscious mind would undoubtedly enhance the power of your conscious mind to make correct choices and decisions when your circumstances require action. If you happen to believe in reincarnation, all your past lifetimes are also stored in your subconscious mind. Some of them may even have a profound influence over your present life.

"The unconscious level:
This is collective - meaning it is not unique and personal. It is like a subconscious level of mind shared by all beings.

Waaii continued, "To have a better understanding of the previous three levels of consciousness, you could use an analogy of a person working with a computer; she or he is the conscious mind sitting in front of the computer, using the keyboard to send commands and to receive their responses on the screen. The hard disk of the computer is the person's subconscious mind where she or he can store all their personal and unique experiences as files, and no one can have access to them but that particular person. The internet is the person's unconscious mind which is shared by all beings.

"The higher conscious level:
This is the subject of your main question and is

unique and personal. It is your connection to the universal mind, Goddess and God. It is your connection to the higher part of who you are and what you are becoming. It stores all the possibilities of your growth, transformation, and transcendence. Even if you do not believe in a god or all of your possibilities, your higher conscious mind does. It is your higher self with the capital S. It is your future selves, waiting patiently for your connection. And here in this garden you are connecting with your higher conscious self. Your higher self was the power behind saving your life."

Cidar was attentively listening as Waaii continued.

"Cidar, before you were reincarnated to your present physical body, you wanted to know the secret of creation. You asked the questions 'Why was the universe created, and by whom? And now you and your higher consciousness, which means us, will work together to address the answer. Your higher self has saved your life for this very reason." Waaii disappeared as fast as he appeared. Cidar came out of the meditation. He was puzzled by the new revelation of his desire to know who created the universe and why. Cidar went home and started collecting his thoughts and writing down what he had learned from Waaii.

Cidar began to internally reflect, "The three levels of consciousness, subconscious, unconscious and the higher conscious levels are there to assist and help our conscious level and us to grow and become more of who we are and what we are becoming. All we need to do is learn how to communicate and work with them; I mean myself. This is something to ponder."

Then Cidar thought to himself, "And I have already succeeded in communicating with my higher consciousness. This is an amazing step forward. And my higher consciousness was that power which saved my life. Furthermore, it wants to work with me to discover who created the universe and why. I may have to set aside my skepticism and doubt and let the process continue. It is indeed a very interesting and exciting undertaking," Cidar thought before he slipped into sleep after a productive day.

6- The Set Avatar: Jamii

The following day as Cidar was walking to work, he ran into Safeer. "Hi, Safeer, I am going to work now. How are you?" Cidar started the conversation.

"I am doing great. How are you? I have not seen you at the temple lately."

Cidar did not want to tell Safeer what he was doing after work, at least not yet. "I am fine. I often go to Mont Taba for a walk after work." Cidar responded

"Would you like to come to my place for tea this afternoon after you get off work?" Safeer asked.

Cidar did not want to say no and have to explain why. He agreed right away and said, "That will be lovely, thank you. I will be there at three thirty."

The back yard of Safeer's house was a well-kept place, with a beautiful garden full of colorful flowers and roses. Their conversation covered different subjects of interest, except Cidar's meditations. He did not want to tell Safeer about them yet. As they were sipping from their teacups, Safeer opened a paper bag, got something out of it, and asked Cidar to extend his arm and open his palm. Cidar followed his instructions. Safeer put in Cidar's palm what looked like seeds of some sort and said, "These are some crushed peanuts. Keep your palm open for a while." Cidar did so without knowing why. After a minute or so, Cidar was surprised to see a blue jay land on his palm and start eating from the crushed peanuts. As Cidar was looking and enjoying the experience, he felt close to that bird and became sad when it flew away. He noticed that the peanuts were almost gone.

Ode to Jay

In a garden of roses, daisies, and carnations,
With dear friends, and a lovely conversation,
Was your journey in its beginning, end, or continuation?

You softly landed on my stretched arm.
With your beaks you tenderly kissed my palm
While pecking your favorite feed.

You felt welcomed,
You felt safe.
Your closeness warmed my heart.
I felt joyous.

Suddenly, you spread your beautiful blue wings,
So blue, like a quiet pond reflecting the sky in a sunny day.
Sadness dropped like a barrel of tar
When you departed and flew away and far.

How I wished
Wingless you were.

Oh my!
You came to seek your favorite seeds
And I wanted you to always be near.

Is it too much to ask
For an equitable deal?

Oh – how selfish I was, no doubt indeed.

The next day in the afternoon Cidar relaxed and went deep into meditation with no trouble. Entering into the rose garden was getting a lot easier to visualize than before. As he was sitting on the chair waiting, a new figure appeared.

"Hi, Cidar, I am Jamii. I am also part of your higher self. Like Waaii I will explain to you the next step to unlocking the mystery of creation." Jamii continued, "This step deals with the mathematical theory of sets and I will try to explain it at a new and deeper level of understanding than you have previously encountered."

Cidar interrupted, "What does the set theory have to do with creation?"

"You will soon understand," Jamii answered as he proceeded. "The set theory states that any objects or numbers which possess similar qualities can be grouped in a set, and the set can be identified by its members' common quality. For example, a set that contains only even numbers is called the set of even numbers. Similarly, the odd number set contains only odd numbers. Moreover, two sets can unite and form a bigger set. The even and odd number sets can be combined and form the all-number set. Now, if we apply our comprehension of consciousness, as Waaii had described it, to the set theory, we can achieve a new and a deeper level of understanding. In the case of the even number set, if we give a consciousness to every even number of the set. We ask what each number would be aware of. The answer is only another even number. In other words, the even numbers of the even-number set are not aware of the existence of odd numbers, because odd numbers are not part of the even number set. However, if we increase the awareness of the even-number set by adding to it odd numbers, then the resulting set is no longer an even-number set. It becomes an all-number set. And we notice that the awareness of the even numbers has increased. Now they are aware of the existence of odd numbers as they have become members of a larger set: the all-number set. Thus their awareness and consciousness has also increased. In a similar fashion, if we apply the set concept to humans, since you now exist in a physical form, you are a member of the physical world. Therefore, you are part of a set called the physical-being set. And you, with your physical senses, are only aware of what is included in the physical-being set. You are not aware of anything that is outside of the physical-being set. However, if any physical being increases her or his awareness that she or he also is a spiritual being, which is a choice they make, then they become part of a larger set called the all-being set. Thus they become more aware and conscious of their true existence, as you, yourself, have accomplished so far. This increased awareness will help you better understand why you exist and who created you."

Cidar now began to realize the relevancy of Jamii's message to the secret of creation. When he arrived home that evening, he wanted to document what he had learned. He started writing in his note book. The pen would not write; it had apparently ran out of ink. Cidar, without thinking, tossed the pen in the waste basket, and while he was trying to pick up another pen, some feeling overwhelmed him, perhaps a feeling of guilt inside him. Since he started to talk and communicate his thoughts to rocks, trees, and spiders, he felt an inner deep feeling of guilt for throwing the empty pen away. He reached to the waste basket and held the pen in his hand and said, "I am so sorry for throwing you away, so sorry. Would you forgive me?" Cidar somehow picked up on what the pen was trying to say to him:

Pen Speaks

They steal the words from me,
They strip me of the images I draw.

They separate me from my
Beloved ink,
Like a lover separated from
The beloved.

They toss me away when empty,
I am hurt,
I cry with no tears.

I am tired of what I do,
I close the shop,
I am out of image-making business,
I quit.
And I will forgive you.

Cidar drew a wide smile on his face and said, "Thank you, pen, I will keep you forever." He held another pen and started writing what he learned that day. He slept well that night.

7- The cell Avatar: Khalia

Cidar was overwhelmed by work in his new position at the restaurant. Each evening, he felt tired and overworked when he got home. He did not have the energy to go to Mont Taba and meditate. One evening he invited his friend Safeer for a cup of tea, reciprocating his invitation of two weeks earlier.

Safeer greeted him, "How are you doing, Cidar? It has been such a long two weeks since we spoke last."

"I am doing great and I am anxious to tell you about my new discoveries," Cidar responded. He felt it was a good time to tell Safeer about his meditations. "I owe it all to you, Safeer," he continued. "I have followed your advice and I am thankful to you. I started meditating more frequently under the tree near Mont Taba. For some time I did not get any answer, and then one day a figure in a human shape appeared and told me he is part of my higher self. I was skeptical at the beginning but then he told me that I was the one who asked him to come when I was looking for the nature of the power that saved my life. I felt more comfortable when I heard that. He told me that my higher self was the power that saved me. And now I am on a new path of discovery which I am not going to tell you yet because

I do not know everything about it. I promise I will share more of my experience when I know more."

"Wow, I am so excited for you, Cidar, and I will be patient till you tell me your new discovery," Safeer respectfully said.

Cidar added, "I look forward to meditating so I can discover more. However, I am very busy now at work. The cook will be back from his vacation to-morrow and then I will somewhat be relieved. For now let us have chocolate cookies and some tea." For the rest of the evening the two friends talked about different subjects of interest. Cidar had a good and restful night after Safeer left.

The next day at three o'clock Cidar headed toward Mont Taba to resume meditation under the tree. Seated within his inner garden, a new figure ap-peared.

"Hi, my name is Khalia and I will be talking to you about your cells."

Cidar interrupted and said, "Not again, another mysterious thing."

"Be patient…." Khalia said. "As your science dis-covered," he continued, "The modern tenets of the Cell Theory include:

1. All known living things are made up of cells.

2. The cell is the structural and functional unit of all living things.

3. All cells come from preexisting cells by division.

4. Cells contain hereditary information which is passed from cell to cell during cell division.

5. All cells are basically the same in chemical composition.

6. All energy flow of life occurs as metabolism and biochemistry within cells.

"Life in the physical plane of existence began inside the cell," Khalia proceeded, "whether it is a single cell organism, like the amoeba or a multi-cell organism. However, when cells learned how to divide and create more cells, they discovered that in order to survive and sustain life, they have to cooperate and help one another. Moreover, microbiologists have recently discovered that every cell in your bodies possesses a level of consciousness and is aware of its environment. In addition, the cell is able to receive instructions from that environment. They call it the science of epigenetics. I would like to add that every newly-created cell is a unique entity in itself. It has a unique consciousness. It can very well decide what path it wants to take and what kind of cells it desires to create. You may remember the Spanish poet Antonio Machado's words *(We do not have a path to walk; we create our own path as we walk.)* So do cells. They make their own paths as they create new cells, independent of their creator cells. Therefore, we can conclude **"The created and the creator are one and the same."**

Khalia disappeared.

Cidar was perplexed over what he had learned and wanted to make sense of the sentence, "The created and the creator are one and the same." It was indeed an overwhelming and puzzling revelation. It made more sense, however, as he pondered, later writing in his journal:

"If I look at cells and how each cell divides into two more cells and each of the newly created cells creates two more cells, then the created cells become the creators of the new cells and so on and so forth. It looks as though the creative energy passes on from the creator to the created. Remarkable; it makes sense!!"

Cidar had, however, a difficult time falling asleep that night. His thoughts were preoccupied by cells and how they behave. He kept tossing and turning for hours without falling asleep. He felt that he was shrinking in size. The longer he tossed and the more he turned, the smaller he got. He felt as small as his DNA. He therefore slipped into a cell of his. As he was exploring through the slime what was inside a cell, he noticed they were called the chromosome pairs. He started counting them. They were twenty-three pairs. "Fantastic, the genealogists were correct," he said to himself. As Cidar continued exploring further, he heard a voice saying, "Hey, you." He turned to where the voice came from and said, "Who is that?"

The voice responded, "I am the next-door neighbor cell."

"You talk down in here," Cidar astonishingly remarked.

"Yes, we do," the cell responded. "We always talk to one another. We even send text messages to each other. We also try to talk to you humans. Sometimes you listen and sometimes you don't. Khalia was actually trying to tell you that we are able to communicate with each other but he suggested to us we tell you in person."

Cidar was stymied. "Well, my goodness. Anything else you would like to tell me, cell?" Cidar said.

"Yes," the cell responded. "I want to recite the following poem on behalf of all cells. OK?"

"Yes, go ahead." Cidar responded.

Cell Speaks

(On behalf of all cells)

In singles or groups we
Always existed.
You made us,
So that
We make you.
Fifty trillions of us
Live inside you in communion.
We survive because
We love one another;
The strong empower the weak -
All is powerful,
The healthy heal the sick -
All is healthy.
Yet,
We are commanded by
Your thoughts, feelings and emotions,
So,
Send us love -
Send us kindness -
Send us compassion,
We -
Send you life.

The cell continued, "And the following is what we (cells) think of life:

Life

Life is a painting,
Courage is the painter.

Life is an art,
Compassion is the artist.

Life is a symphony,
Love is the composer.

Life is beautiful,
You are the beauty.

Life is a state of
Growing and becoming.

Life is sweet, when
You accept its bitterness.

Cidar looked at the cell as he was wiping off tears from joyful clouded eyes, with unspoken gratitude and knelt with respect for all cells. He found himself back in bed with the desire to be engulfed in sleep.

8- The Energy Avatar: Tagha

"Hi Cidar, I am Tagha and I will be talking with you about energy," Tagha said as she appeared, sitting in the other chair in front of Cidar.

"Well, that is something more relevant to the subject of creation," Cidar responded, as his gaze captivated by the beautiful female figure.

"I am glad you feel this way; now we are starting to deepen our conversation," Tagha said as she proceeded, "Everything or no-thing, whatever or whoever exists, has a level of energy associated with its existence. The consciousness or the awareness-level of an entity depends on the level of energy they exist in, whether the consciousness is conscious or unconscious of its existence. We, your higher self, exist in a higher-energy reality than your physical world (not more energy, but a different kind of energy). Most of you physical beings are not aware and conscious of our existence. But we do exist and are aware of our existence in the higher energy reality and are aware of yours as well. Even though the awareness of your conscious level exists now in the lowest of the Low- Energy Reality, you and we, your higher self, are one and the same entity as Waaii explained earlier. Now you are aware of us because you made the effort to communicate. We are here to help you and assist you in your growth. We responded to your request. We do not interfere without your permission. We wait and patiently wait for you to ask us, and you did. You, Cidar, have become a member of a larger set of beings. You are aware of both your physical and spiritual existences and you are, with some effort, able to communicate between these two existences."

"It is nice to hear that," Cidar respectfully nodded.

"It is indeed true," Tagha said.

As she was about to proceed, Cidar interrupted her and said, "Before we continue, I would like to clarify something you said, that our physical world is the lowest of the Low-Energy Reality. Are there any other worlds of the Low-Energy Reality?"

"Yes, what we call, the astral, causal, and faith. I will explain later what they mean. But now let us talk about the definition of energy. A simple definition: "Energy can be defined as the ability to do work. Our thoughts, including yours, are energy because there is work to do when we think. In your physical world there are many different levels of energy: chemical elements and materials can be described by their unique level of energy. Their molecules vibrate with certain frequencies, thus creating a level of energy unique to their existence. Rocks are the lowest level of energy because their molecules vibrate with lowest sustainable frequency, whereas gas-like elements vibrate with the highest sustainable frequency. Thus, it has the highest energy level of the sustainable physical materials."

"I have a question," Cidar interrupted. "You said previously that everything, as well as no-things can have a certain level of energy associated with their existence. How could no-things exist?"

"They exist because there is a certain level of energy associated with their existence," Tagha answered. "Let me explain. In your universe there are vastly more no-things than actual things. Roughly 74 percent of the universe is no-thing or what physicists call Dark Energy; 22 percent is dark matter, particles you cannot see. Only 4 percent is baryonic matter, the stuff you can see. Even some-thing is mostly no-thing; atoms overwhelmingly consist of empty space. If you imagine an atom the size of this beautiful rose garden, then the nucleus is a small speck in the middle of the garden with few electrons orbiting the nucleus. The rest of the atom is empty space. It has no-thing in it. Yet it has energy associated with it. In 1998, astronomers measuring the expansion of the universe determined that dark energy, no-thing energy, is pushing apart the universe at an ever-accelerating speed. Meaning, the dark energy, no-thing energy, is much greater than the gravitational energy that pulls galaxies closer. The discovery of no-thing and its ability to influence the fate of the cosmos is considered the most important astronomical finding of the past decade." Tagha stopped for few seconds to give Cidar some time to absorb what has been said. Cidar took several deep breaths and said nothing.

Tagha asked, "May I continue?"

"Go ahead, I am OK." Cidar responded.

"Now I would like to postulate the following," Tagha continued. "Energy can exist in no-thing-ness. Thought is energy. Thought is the first energy you exert when you want to create something. We would call this energy feminine energy. An action might follow a thought. The action is called masculine energy. We would, therefore, claim that in any creative process we start with feminine energy, the inactive part, followed by masculine energy, the active part. An example: Just before Michelangelo sculpted the statue of David, and when he saw the marble rock, he thought that David was inside the rock. That was his feminine energy. Then when he held the chisel and started chiseling the rock to uncover David, that was his masculine energy. These two types of energy exist in all living things, regardless of species or gender.

"Finally, suppose you are able by your own thought, to lower the energy of an object, a bottle of water for instance. You would get ice. Now, in order to sustain the ice in the bottle for a very long time, you must put the bottle in a freezer, otherwise, it will go back to water. We would thus conclude that when we lower the energy of a system we must have space to contain and sustain the newly-achieved energy level. Otherwise, the system will go back to its original high-energy level, which is the default state."

"I have to digest what you have shared with me and think more about it," Cidar murmured.

"In case you have more questions, you know you can always ask us," Tagha followed. "Now going back to answering your earlier question; there are four planes of existence in the Low-Energy Reality:

"**Physical:** It begins from the time you are born and ends at the time you drop your physical body. Time and space play a big part in its conscious aware-ness. Like I said, it is the lowest form of energy in the Low-Energy Reality. It is also your choice and decision to experience this level of existence. No God or anyone else chooses or decides for you.

"**Astral:** It is the level you experience when you drop your physical body. It is similar to the physical plane in consciousness but relatively higher in energy (different amount or different nature of energy). Time and space do not exist.

"**Causal:** It is where cause and effect take place. It is a conscious reality where thoughts are instantaneously created. It is more fluid and flexible than the physical and the astral planes. It is easier to get into from the astral plane than from the physical plane.

"**Faith:** It is where you store everything you believe in, whether it comes from religions or your own privately created beliefs. It is the highest energy level of the Low-Energy Reality.

"I would, also, like to explain why we call these levels of existence Low-Energy Reality. It is because they all share in common a very distinctive attribute, namely duality.

"Meaning, your consciousness chooses from dual reality to manifest. Whatever you experience emotionally, its opposite is automatically also manifested. It is up to you which side of emotions you tap into. The following are some of the examples of a world of duality:

Hope -- Despair
Good health -- Disease

Knowledge -- Ignorance
Love -- Hate
Joy -- Sorrow
Wealth -- Poverty
Courage – Fear
Good -- Evil
Angels -- Devils
Dominion -- Domination

"For example, if you encounter a situation in your world that requires courage to deal with, then fear is also created alongside courage. And it is totally up to you as to which side of the dual energies you would consider to act upon, courage or fear. I would suggest courage. You could also think of a world free of duality by seeing both sides as one. As Rumi said," *(I have put duality away and see the two worlds as one.)*

"The High-Energy Reality (HER), on the other hand, is a non-dual state of consciousness. It can only be expressed through one level of energy - LOVE."

"Tagha, I have a question to ask," Cidar interrupted. "You labeled dominion as a positive energy and domination as a negative one. Why are they different? "

"I am glad you asked this question," Tagha responded. "In the physical world when an individual or a group of people become powerful, they tend to have power over the weak, In HER we, empower the weak so that they become powerful. In your language, there are no words to distinguish between the two sets of energy. To show the difference we examine the two words that you are familiar with: dominion for empowerment and domination for power over and control."

"Wow, Thank you Tagha for explaining the difference." Cidar excitingly commented. Tagha smiled with satisfaction as she disappeared.

9- The Deity Avatar: Sama

"It is a lie - any talk of God that does not comfort you."
                    Meister Eckhart (1260-1328)

"I have lived on the lip of insanity
Wanting to know reason.
Knocking on a door, it opens
I have been knocking from the inside."
                    Rumi

Cidar found that he was learning more every day from his inner world than his outer world. As he wrote and thought more about what he learned, he was increasingly appreciative of his surroundings. The information he was gaining from his inner world had a profound impact on his personality and his character. He became more loving, more compassionate, and more honest. He started looking at things and people around him with deeper and more thoughtful insight, with an eye for what lies hidden beneath the surface. He began gaining a broader view and a deeper understanding of why life events, fate, tragedy, and luck are the way they are. People whom he worked with noticed how he softened his demeanor and his association with each and every one of them. They also found he was more pleasant and easier to work with.

My Inner World

My inner world is where
My outer world originates.

My self-esteem is nurtured
In my inner world.

My inner world is never validated
By my outer world.

My inner world must be peaceful
For my outer world to be in peace.

My self-confidence is enforced
In my inner world.

I simply am my inner world.

One evening, when Cidar returned home, he was
shocked to find a swarm of ants on his open sugar
bowl on his kitchen counter. He quickly reached for
the anti-ant spray to kill them. Some inner twitch
stopped him from spraying. He was about to com-
mit murder by spraying these ants. He thought
of how he was able to save the spider's life. The
ants were no different. He carried the whole bowl
with the ants in it to the hallway outside his studio
and let them enjoy their meal. "Naturally, the ants
will come back inside the studio when they run
out of sugar," he thought. A brilliant idea came to

his mind. If he would always leave grains of sugar outside his studio, then the ants would not need to come inside his kitchen to look for food, and he would not be bothered with them. When he slept that night, he dreamed of group of ants thanking him for saving their lives and providing food for them.

As he was walking toward Mont Taba and the tree to meditate the next afternoon, he thought of his utmost connection with everything around him. Even though he was walking alone, he felt he was not alone. The ants and other creatures were walking along with him.

The Divine Walk

I walk alone,
So they say.

I look up,
The stars,
The moon, and
The sun walk along.

I look down,
The ants,
The worms and
The beetles crawl along.

I look around,
The crows,

The nightingale and
The sandpipers fly along.

Walk not alone,
So says the divine.

A very beautiful and radiant female figure appeared sitting on the adjacent chair in the rose garden. "Hello Cidar, my name is Sama, and . . ."

Before she continued, Cidar, stunned by her beauty, could not hide his feeling, and said, "You are so beautiful Sama. I have not seen a beauty like yours."

Sama responded, "Just remember, Cidar, I am you and I am your inner world. Your inner world appears more beautiful to you as you continue your connection with it. We are pleased to continue working with you, and that work will increase the level of our beauty. We would also like to commend you for saving the lives of the ants and the spider. " Cidar painted a grateful smile on his face. Sama continued, "Now, I would like to talk to you about the deity. Your physical world has for too long existed in dark clouds of fear, guilt, and lack of trust. The strong and the rich dominate the weak and the poor. Your personal relationships and how you relate to one another have also been infected by these dark clouds. The reason, we believe, is the image that you dearly hold of the deity. Theologians, undoubtedly, have made important contributions to clarify the image of God, yet thousands of religious people continue to imprison, torture, and persecute in the name of a frightening image of the deity. These practices emanate from antiquated concepts of God that are embedded very deep in your sub-conscious minds. For your self-improvement and healing of your world, you need to re-image the deity. This process must go beyond talk; you must fully live, love, breathe, and embrace the new im-age. I will show how you easily can achieve that change, improve yourselves and thereby heal your world."

"Why would that be so relevant -- changing the im-age of the deity when wanting to unlock the secret of creation?" Cidar interrupted.

Sama responded, "The new image will pave the way to a deeper realization and understanding of how creation came about. You will better understand this later, if you allow me to proceed."

"Please, continue," Cidar said, filled with great ex-pectation.

Sama continued, "In your world you refer to the word 'God' so much. The term has many differ-ent meanings and images. One image of God that was imposed upon you can be traced back to your childhood. If you remember, Cidar, as a child, your mother told you about God as an old man with a white beard. He sits above in heaven, punishing people who go astray, destroying cities whenever he feels like it and rewarding others who follow his message in the Bible, the Torah, or the Quran. That image frightened you and made it hard for you to urinate."

"Yes I do remember," Cidar replied.

Sama went on, "Sanctuaries and houses are built to worship this image out of fear. Individuals of authority force others to believe in it to gain control and dominance. Millions of people are being killed to protect this image. Many of you want to continue to hold to this image with its conditions, guilt, and limitations that are imposed upon you by your misinterpreted religions."

"What do you mean by misinterpreted religions?" Cidar interrupted.

Sama responded with a calm voice, "In the Bible, both the old and the new testaments, and in the Quran God has been interpreted as compassionate, merciful, kind, forgiving, and loving. At the same time, God is seen as a destroyer and punisher. A consciousness which possesses this kind of duality can only exist in the Low-Energy Reality. The image of hell and heaven would also be confined by the Low-Energy Reality state of consciousness. Therefore, the holy books were only interpreted by the mindset of the Low-Energy Reality. We, in the higher energy reality or HER, think they are misinterpretations. We believe the energy of the deity exists in the higher level of the HER. Our interpretation of good and evil, heaven and hell is merely a state of mind that Low-Energy Reality consciousness experiences. For example, if a person commits an evil deed, his guilt is interpreted as hell. Similarly, if he does a good deed, his joy and euphoria are interpreted as heaven. In other words, good and evil, heaven and hell can only exist inside the mindset of Low-Energy Reality; calmness and clarity are the products of feeling good and thinking of heaven. Confusion, chaos, and disturbance of clarity are the products of evil and hell. We, in HER, do not believe in good and evil or in heaven and hell. It will even be clearer when I explain the attributes of the new image of the deity."

After a brief pause, Sama continued, "Some people want to distance themselves from these old pictures of God. They end up shutting God out, becoming atheists or agnostics, thus creating a void in their reality they are unable to fill. Subsequently, their lives become hollow, misdirected, or purposeless."

"I would try to fill the void and suggest the following image of the deity so your lives can be full of richness, purpose, happiness, and success, without guilt. Though it is hard to adequately define a multidimensional level of existence with a two- dimensional language such as yours, I will try to simplify the concept. I define God as pure love. When I experience pure love, I create no fear; I do not judge; I do not punish; I do not dominate; and I do not destroy. Therefore, God is a level of energy which purely loves. It means you must believe in God out of love, not fear, because you know for certain that God does not judge, does not punish, does not dominate, does not destroy, and, above all, does not seek to control. I know it is hard for those who seek to dominate and control in the name of God to accept such an image. Rumi has in fact warned you of the danger of such a belief when he said:

> 'You talk to me a lot of God, and every time
> You make me feel guilty. But watch it,
> This word is going to poison you if you
> Use it to have power over me.'

"So, if you give yourselves the opportunity to accept the notion that God has loved, does love, and will always love you no matter what you do and think, and if you open up to receiving that love and own it, then you, in turn, could pass the love first to yourself, second to others, and third to the world at large. Thus, your realities can be filled with a sense of purpose, richness, happiness, and success."

Sama looked around the rose garden, admired the red, white, and yellow roses, looked affectionately towards Cidar and continued, "In our search, as your higher self, for the true deity of God, we have glimpsed the deity of the Goddess, a tiny glimpse perhaps, but a glimpse nonetheless. That glimpse has opened the door to the rebirth of the Goddess energy. I say rebirth because her energy has always been in existence, you just were not aware of it. In truth, you even tried to shut it completely out of your consciousness in believing, promoting, and protecting ideology in the form of religions that focus only on the masculine part and completely ignore the feminine part. The rebirth of the Goddess has allowed us to rediscover our own meaning of our feminine energy as well as rediscovering a more complete and useful definition of God. The feminine energy is the creative and the nurturing energy. It is the energy that brings balance and harmony. Your present world is in a pressing need of these qualities: creativity, nurturing, balance and harmony. You have throughout history misunderstood the feminine energy and how to use it in your daily life. The reason for this misunderstanding is not that you are ignorant of its existence, but rather you always have lived in a male-dominant society. Your personal religions throughout the world have forced upon you the image of the deity as being all masculine in form of God, Allah, and Jehovah and completely ignored the feminine energy. As the God energy gives pure love so does the Goddess energy. In fact, the combination of both would indeed give greater pure love and greater energy than each alone. Hence, the whole is greater than the sum of its parts. This combination has formed what you call in Islam "ALLAH", in Christianity "JEHOVAH", in Judaism "YAHWE.

"I am going to stop here and conclude our meeting. Next time we meet I will explain the nature and the attributes of these energies," Sama said with a smile as she disappeared.

Cidar came out of the meditation, feeling vibrant and refreshed. He was very excited about what Sama, the most beautiful of women, had told him. He was impatient for tomorrow to connect with her again. As he walked back home, he was dancing and singing with joy and excitement he had never experienced before. When he approached his home, he noticed the neighbor's gray and white cat sitting on the stairs leading to his studio. He held her in his arms as she meowed a welcoming sound.

Boosy the Cat

Paws of gray and white,
Softly pawing on my side,
Sounding,
Meow Meow Meow,
I hear;

Love   Love   Love.
When love is wordless,
Love is vast.

*

The next day, as soon as Cidar sat down on his chair in the rose garden, Sama appeared on the other chair and with excitement and joy began right where she had ended her conversation "Now let me explain further the nature and the attributes of the feminine and the masculine energies, which are essential to forming the whole which you call ALLAH or JEHOVAH or YAHWE," Sama proceeded.

"The Attributes of the God energy

"It has no desire to reward or punish: God does not need to reward anyone for doing good and positive deeds because he knows that the self-satisfaction and peaceful and tranquil feelings generated as a result of doing good deeds are ample rewards. These feelings are what God meant by heaven. Similarly God does not need to punish anyone for doing bad and evil deeds, because he knows that evil people punish themselves by having guilty consciences and consequently, they lead unhappy and miserable lives and coping with dark energies that last through their soulful journeys. These lives and dark energies are what God meant by hell.

"It has no desire to interfere: God does not wish to interfere in your and our world because he has great respect for all of us. He knows that we can solve and handle our own problems.

"It has desire to help when asked: God is willing, however, to help but only when asked, because he has respect. To our great surprise, he usually gives help in his own mysterious way.

"It has dominion, not domination: As Tagha mentioned the difference between dominion and domination, I, however, would like to elaborate further on the meaning and how it relates to God. As you know and as Tagha previously said, the words domination and dominion in the dictionary have similar meanings. In HER we would like to differentiate between the two to help explain our point. Domination is exercising control and power over someone or something. When a person feels powerful, she or he usually likes to have power over a less powerful person and force the less powerful person to submit to her or his will. Dominion, on the other hand, would empower the less power-ful person instead of overpowering her or him. When a person feels powerful, she or he would seek to empower the less powerful person so that both would be equally powerful. God seeks to have dominion.

"It does not forgive: God does not need to forgive because he knows there are no sins to forgive.

Sacred Secret

I once visited my house of worship,
God holding a chalice of wine,
Intoxicated,
A sacred secret slurred.

"Nothing to forgive,
Nothing to judge,
Nothing to feel guilty about
Because
There is no sin."

Oh my!
How wisely
Intoxicating.

"It does not judge: God does not need to judge because he has clarified the difference between good and evil and the consequences of doing either one.

"It is always seeking to know more of itself: God is dynamic energy, is always changing and growing.

"It is loving and peaceful, and has no form."

Path to God

This path to God
Made me such
An old sweet beggar.

I was starving
Until one night
My love tricked God himself
To fall into my bowl,

Now Hafiz in infinitely rich,

But all I ever want to do
Is keep emptying out
My emerald filled pockets
Upon this tear stained world.

Hafiz

"I do not want to trick God to fall into my bowl, as Hafiz did. My God has always been in my bowl. I have just realized it. And this world not only has tears, but it also has joy."

God

You have always been in my bowl.

The joy and the tears of this world
Have uncovered my bowl.

Now,

I am well fed,
I am rich,

And,

Your love for me dissolves
My arrogant-self.

"Who is this God that dissolves my arrogant-self?"

My God

My God does not punish,
Nor does he reward.

My God does not have heaven,
Nor does he have hell.

My God does not forgive.
Nor does he judge.

My God does not fight evil;
He knows that evil ultimately transforms itself.

My God is not static.
My God is dynamic.

My God is always growing and expanding.
My God is always discovering more of himself.

My God always loves me
Regardless of what I do.

My God has great respect for me;
He does not interfere without my permission.

My God is light,
My God is Love.

"The attributes of the Goddess energy:

"It has no desire to be a singular authority: Goddess energy chooses not to be authoritarian, even though it has the power to do so.

"It has no desire to have supremacy: The Goddess does not need to be superior.

"It has no desire to be absolute: Goddess likes to share her power with God. The communion of Goddess and God forms ALLAH-JEHOVAH-YAHWEH.

"Similar to God:

"It has no desire to dominate.
It is always seeking to know more of itself.
It is the source of all creation. She is the mother of all mothers.
It is loving and peaceful and it is formless."

My Goddess

My Goddess is the mother and
The source of all creations.

Through her womb
God was conceived.

Through her love and communion
With God I was created.

As an entity of consciousness I live on,
Embraced by her love and kindness.

Her light is what I seek
And the reason for my growth.

Her compassion folds my existence
To eternity.

Her love for me is greater than all the love
In all hearts combined.

My goddess is the candle
That lights my way home.

Dance

I shyly approached the being
Of my desire,
Held her hands to accompany me

To the dance floor.
Danced a whole series of
Spirited, melodic waltzes,
Returned her to her seat,
Took my leave with
A courtly bow.

I just touched the Goddess.

Harmonia Mundus

Two-thirty in the morning, I woke up,
A musical band vibrantly playing
Next to my bed.

The soprano-chanting star,
The tenor-voiced earth,
And the drum of the silver moon
Joined in.

Echoing across the universe,
A song of love.

Mankind would be a lot happier
If they took a few music lessons
From the greatest composers of all-
Goddess and God

Cidar began to drift away, pondered the new image of the deity and recalled the love he had for his dad, his mother, his wife, and his children, and how much he missed them. Sama sensed his wandering thoughts and wanted to bring him back to the present.

She said, "Now I'd like to talk about feminine energy." Cidar brought his attention back to what she was saying. She continued, "How do we utilize our feminine energy? First of all feminine energy has nothing to do with being female. It exists in both females and males. What is the feminine energy? It is the energy you use when you:

"1- Think, have thoughts
  2- Feel
  3- Give birth to new ideas
  4- Open up to receiving

"These four actions are undoubtedly available to both men and women. You are all able to think, feel, give birth to new ideas, and able to receive. The Goddess energy adds pure love to these actions. The motivator behind your ability to think, feel, give birth to new ideas, and receive, I would suggest, is love, pure love. This is how you revive the Goddess energy in your daily life. You allow pure love to be the motivator behind your thoughts, feelings, creativity, and perception. To revive the true and complete God energy (not the Bible's, Torah's or the Quran's) is to make pure love as your motivator for everything you do; actual-

izing your thoughts, feelings, new ideas and ability to receive. These two energies - the masculine
God energy and the feminine Goddess energy are
indeed available to all of you, regardless of gender. When you search for spiritual connection and
evolution, you need to be open to receiving the
great and pure love these two energies have stored
for you. What I mean by you is, all of you; miner-
als, plants, animals and humans. Begin to co-create
your realities with all of them in mind."

Cidar had listened with great interest and pondered
the word love. "I would like to ask you if you could
define 'LOVE'," Cidar said to Sama.

"I have sensed that you would ask such a question!"
Sama replied with a smile. "What is LOVE? The
question now is: How do we define LOVE? Even
though the definition of love may be personal in
its nature and practice and may differ from one
person to another, we, nonetheless, may always
seek some common and universal definition of
love. Love not only is a feeling and an emotion, but
it is also a skill. Playing the piano is a skill which
requires daily practice. So does love. Therefore, we
need to follow certain steps and practice every day
to improve our loving nature. We, your higher self,
would suggest the following steps:

"1- **Care** for yourselves (self-love) and for others.

Question how beneficial your actions are to yourselves and to others.

"2- **Know** yourselves and others. Approach every situation with the desire to learn. Be open to understanding.

"3- **Respect** yourselves and others by honoring your emotions and others' emotions. Try to process your emotions in a positive way, no matter how negative they may be.

"4- **Be responsible** for yourselves and be responsive to others. You need to take full responsibility for the reality you create. You also need to be responsive to others in dealing with their realities rather than being responsible for their realities.

"5- **Create a space for change**. Without being judgmental, allow yourselves to change and create the space for others to change.

"6- **Have the courage to be honest.** Be brutally honest with yourselves and admit your mistakes to yourselves. Be diplomatically and tactfully honest with others.

"7- **Give to yourselves and others**. Give the best to yourselves and to others without expecting anything in return.

"8- **Open up to receiving.** Be open to receive when giving is offered and be thankful.

"9- **Keep what you promise** to yourselves and others.

"10- **Be grateful** and allow the gratitude to change you to be better to yourselves and others.

"When you practice these steps in your daily life, then you allow the Goddess and God energies to be part of your existence and to help you co-create the world you desire to have and experience. These steps are not in any way absolute. You may create your own steps, or you could add or omit any step you wish, and have your own personal definition of love."

Sama smiled as she disappeared. Cidar wanted to thank her for her illuminating insights. He said; "Thank you," a second late after her departure. She, nonetheless, heard him. He knew that.

Love Animated

Oh God!
I have found
Love.

I drop
The confusion,
The worry,
And the doubt.

I now care,
Respect,
Respond,
And seek to
Know.

I allow,
I give,
I receive.

I am honest,
I keep promises
And
I am grateful.

10- The Universe Avatar: Konna

"No need to go to faraway places in order to travel."
Ibrahim Ibn Salma

Cidar took some time off from meditating to reflect what he had learned thus far. He began to write down everything as he received it, without any intrusion of his own thoughts and feelings. He took a two-week vacation from his work to have neither distraction nor interruption. He had a prior feeling that whatever was coming next would be very important and would require his full attention and focus. One day when the sun was bright and the air was relatively warm, he found himself headed to Mont Taba, where he hugged and made himself comfortable under the usual tree and started to meditate.

Next to his chair in the rose garden a new female figure appeared. She was stunningly beautiful, far more beautiful than Sama. Cidar wildly opened his inner eyes as he was gently struck by her beauty and said, "My God, you are so beautiful. You are even more beautiful than Sama."

"Yes Cidar. Your inner world is getting even more beautiful now. My name is Konna and I will be trying to answer your questions about who created the universe and why it was created." Her voice sounded like a romantic symphony that cleansed his heart and mind. Cidar fell silent, listened with rapt attention. "What you know so far and Tagha described the four assumptions that we must keep in mind about energy as we proceed," Konna said. "I would like to briefly go over them again:

"1- There is a tremendous amount of energy in nothingness.

2- Feminine energy is the creative energy.

3- Feminine energy is the first energy you use to create followed by masculine energy.

4- Finally, low energy needs a space to be sustainable.

"Based on what you have previously learned together with the four assumptions of energy, we may be able to construct a story of what might have happened as creation came into being. Using your imagination to attempt to unlock the mystery could be your first step. Albert Einstein has already said that imagination is more important than knowledge. What he meant was that imagination is always limitless while knowledge is limited. In addition, the Spanish poet Antonio Mechado declared that you are the path-walker: You do not have a path to walk, but you make your own path as you walk. It means, as Barack Obama said, "Our destiny is not written for us but is written by us," which can only be true when the creator and the created are one and the same. I will take you, Cidar, on a journey through which the only provision you need is your imagination."

Traveler

Traveler whose sole provision is
Imagination.

Thinking ahead, the mind knows
Where to go;
Looking ahead, the eyes see
The way;
Soaring ahead, the soul enriches
The journey.

*

Heart touched by love,
Surrendering.

Mountains bow to his presence;
Valleys rise to greet him;

A weaver of his destiny,
A maker of his odyssey,
A magical traveler.

11- The Story

"The universe is made of stories, not of atoms."
                    Poet Muriel Rukeyser

This is one of them.

The beautiful Konna continued, "For a few moments let us have an open mind and try to explore the mystery. After all, a mind is like a parachute; it would not be useful unless it is fully open."

Konna took a deep breath before she continued, "At the beginning, before anything ever existed, before anything was ever conceived, there was no-thing. And out of no-thing a form of energy was born - energy so beautiful, so peaceful, so loving, so radiant, and so vibrant, I would call this energy the feminine energy (anima), which gave rise to the Goddess energy. Tagha has previously mentioned in detail the attributes of the Goddess energy. I would like to briefly go over them:

"1- It has no desire to be a singular authority.
2- It has no desire to have supremacy.
3- It has no desire to be absolute.
4- It has no desire to dominate.
5- It is loving and peaceful.
6- It always seeks to know more of itself.
7- It is the source of all creation.
8- It is formless.

"Because of these attributes and the desire to share, the Goddess gave birth to God out of her womb, figuratively speaking, so that she would have company. God gave, in turn, the rise to the masculine energy (animus), which has the following attributes:

"1- It has no desire to reward or punish.
2- It has no desire to interfere.
3- It has desire to help when asked.
4- It has dominion not domination.
5- It does not forgive.
6- It does not judge.
7- It always seeks to know more of itself.
8- It is loving and peaceful.
9- It is formless.

"Goddess and God communed, and out of this communion you were born: What I mean by 'you' is all that ever exists. At the beginning of your existence, you were unaware and unconscious of who you were, where you came from, and where you were going. In other words, you were unconscious of your reality. I would identify you at that stage of your existence as an 'entity of unconsciousness'; your unconscious mind was ruling your existence. However, you as a collective unconscious had a couple of good things going for you- your ability to generate thoughts and your curiosity to know. Therefore, you asked the questions:

Who are we?
Where do we come from? and,
Where are we going?."

Cidar paid even closer attention, feeling that the questions, 'who created the universe and why' would soon be answered.

Konna continued uninterrupted, "Since you existed in a very high level of energy and without being able to make sense of your existence you thought, what if you lower your energy?. Perhaps you may have a glimpse of the answers or may touch some of their essence and simply have a better understanding of your existence. So you did, but you were unable to sustain the lower level of energy and by default you returned to the higher level. You tried again and again, and the results were the same. You finally realized that you needed a space to contain the lower level of energy and thus sustain its level.

"However, you had no clue as to how to create the space, so you asked for help. Goddess and God responded and offered their assistance. You specifically asked them to help you create the space. Had you asked them the original magical questions - who are you? where do you come from? and where are you going?, they would happily have answered you, and your task would have been complete. But you did not. Since they do not judge and they have great respect for you, they were delighted to help you create the space. They would, however, have helped create the space with you but not for you. The space and what would have been in it had to be of your own making and creation. Goddess and God would not decide what kind of space or what kind of stuff it would be filled with. They basically did not wish to interfere and instruct you as to what to do. You, the created, became the creator, as the Avatar Khalia told you. So you accepted; you all diligently worked, and the space was created.

"Your first task was to lower your energy and see if it could be contained and sustained in the newly created space. You did and it worked. You were excited, jumping all over the space with joy. However, it was not much of a jump because you came in as gas-like energy and were still transparent in reality. Since, at this stage of your existence, you had such a great experience in your ability to lower your energy and create the space to contain it, that you went ahead without hesitation and did it, and you became water. However, you discovered that water needed a space to contain and sustain its level of energy due to its fluidity. You lowered your energy even further, and you became ice. You lowered it even further, and you became a rock. Then, you discovered that a rock could be a space to contain and sustain water. Remember you are path-walkers; you have no given path to follow, but you make and create your own path as you walk. As you were trying to experience and familiarize yourselves with all these intricate levels of energy which you just discovered, you encountered even deeper and more sophisticated levels of energy within the water that would eventually give rise to life. You decided you wanted to experience these levels. In order to do so you needed a space to contain them and sustain them. This space was the manifestation of the physical bodies.

"As you looked around, you noticed that the space was still empty, just you and your thoughts. You made the decision to fill it with the newly-discovered levels of energy: gas, water and rocks. Therefore, you generated the Big Bang. And you did that for one reason and one reason only - to fill the space and nothing more. You discovered to your amazement that more unexpected things happened:

"Heat generation!
  Chemical reaction!
  Light emission!
  Star birth and
  Galaxy formation!.

"And the universe as you know it now started to take shape. More than that, something magical happened: you became aware of your conscious mind. Up to then your existence was ruled by your unconscious mind. The Big Bang shook the core of your existence and awakened your conscious mind. You looked around and at each other. You noticed some of you were bright stars, others were dim, small galaxies and others were big. Your ego was born; you were a bright star. Another was a dwarf; you were a big galaxy with a billion stars; others were small with only a million stars. You became individually separate.

"The collective unconsciousness became a separate consciousness. Some of you made the decision to go back to the higher energy reality and discover your own way to know the answers to the three questions with no involvement in the creation of the universe. Others (you are one of them) decided to be planets around stars where life can be sustained. Earth-like planets started to form. You discovered that most of these creative processes took a very long time to develop. Time became part of your newly-created reality, and you became part of time and space continuum. The earth-like planets developed to become a space to contain and sustain life as you know it today. And as your ego evolved, so did your individual and separate spaces which contained the life of plants, animals, and humans.

You had also discovered that trees, animal, and human bodies as spaces could not contain and sustain life forever. They grew and decayed, and you must leave them and create new ones. The birth, death, and rebirth cycle was planted in your conscious and subconscious minds."

Konna paused for a short time and looked at Cidar's eyes, sensed how deeply attentive he was and continued, "You have been in this cycle of death and rebirth for thousands of years, as you can see in figure 1. And through the process you have forgotten the original reasons you were experiencing this physical reality. You even thought that this cycle is all there ever was, ever is, and ever will be. You have also forgotten the original attributes of Goddess and God. You completely dismissed the idea of the Goddess and created God out of your self-image which is controlled by your ego: tyrant, punisher, egotistical, forgiving, rewarding, judging and also loving."

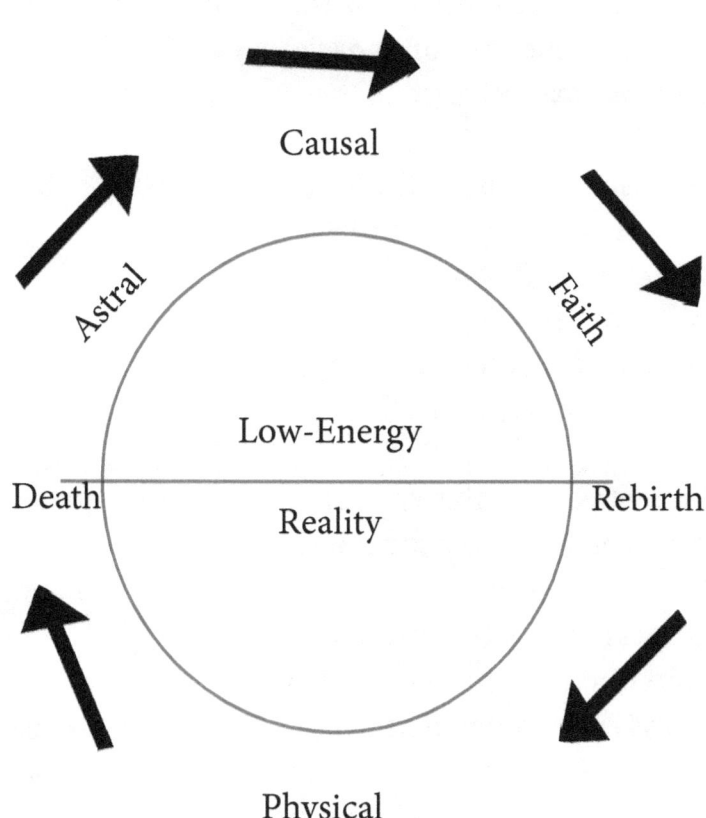

Figure 1

Planes of Existence
in the Low-Energy Reality

"Now you ask again the original questions: Who created the universe and why?
You, as a consciousness, have created the universe, even though you were unconscious of it because your unconscious mind was then ruling your existence. As a collective unconscious you decided to create this vast universe.

"The reason you did it was to find the answers to the following three questions:

"1- Who are you?
  2- Where did you come from?
  3- Where are you going?

"If I may take the liberty of answering these questions, I would answer them as follows:
"1- You are entities or sparks of consciousness always seeking to know more of yourselves.
"2- You unconsciously came from no-thing. The Goddess created herself from no-thing. She created God from her womb. Goddess and God had a communion to achieve a greater whole, which is greater than the sum of its parts. You were born as a part of this whole.
"3- You are consciously going back to no-thingness and along the way you become aware and conscious of everything. I emphasize the word consciously, when you left the reality of no-thingness you were unconscious of your existence; now, when

you decide to go back, you become aware and conscious of every step you traverse to get back. "

Konna paused a moment, wrapped her beautiful turquoise scarf around her shoulders and continued, "Cidar, I will stop now to give you time to digest what I have said thus far. I will meet you here tomorrow." Then she disappeared.

Before he went to sleep that night, Cidar thought that his participation in creating this universe was indeed a monumental discovery that never had before crossed his mind. Even though he did it collectively, he still felt proud of his accomplishments. He fell asleep as he was wondering about his next step.

12- Coming Home

"I am at home. Why are you not here?"
                                    Hafiz

Konna greeted Cidar cheerfully: "Welcome back, Cidar."

Cidar responded with a welcoming bow.

Konna continued, "We sensed you were wondering about your next step; you can see that you now have a choice to make, Cidar. You either decide to continue to exist in the Low-Energy Reality, the world of duality, have several future lifetimes and experience the cycle of death and rebirth over and over with the suffering associated with it, or move into the High-Energy Reality (HER) with a giant step forward, closer to Goddess and God. Each and every one of you will ultimately decide to move into HER, but the question is when? Since you are the only ones to decide, Goddess and God will never decide for you; why not choose to take that step now? Many of you are attached to what the material and physical world has to offer and want to continue experiencing the nature of its inherent duality, as we mentioned earlier. Others are longing to achieve a non-dual world of existence which can only be fulfilled in HER. In HER all emotions except love drop because of their heaviness. Love is the only emotion that could rise to the High Energy Reality. As you can see in Figure 2, all beings that are conscious of HER experience absolute and unconditional love." Konna paused.

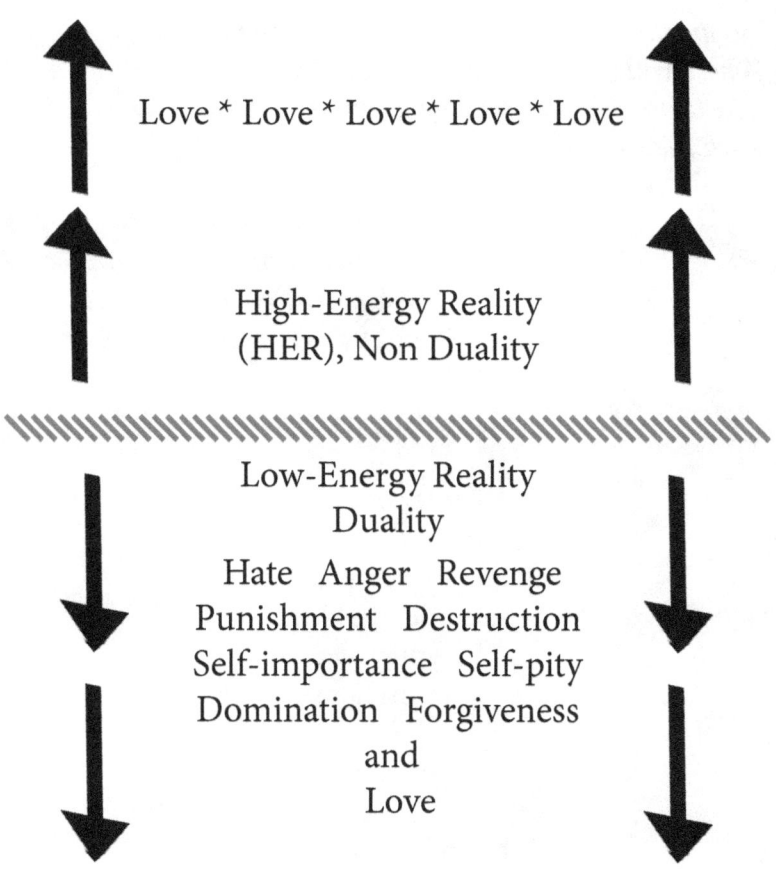

Love * Love * Love * Love * Love

High-Energy Reality
(HER), Non Duality

Low-Energy Reality
Duality

Hate   Anger   Revenge
Punishment   Destruction
Self-importance   Self-pity
Domination   Forgiveness
and
Love

Figure 2

*"I come from elsewhere, and though I do not know where
that is, I am certain to return there in the end. When I die,
I will soar with angels, and when I die to the angels, what I
shall become, you cannot imagine."*

Rumi

*"So journey my friend to the beloved Allah,
Where you find your eternal home.
Like drops of water seeking to unite
With the vast ocean of bliss."*

*Omer AL-Khayamm
Translated from Farsi   to Arabic
By Ahmed Rami, and from Arabic
To English by Ibrahim Ibn Salma*

Coming Home

I - water of the sea,
I - vapor, I rise,
I – clouds above the mountains,
I experience, I learn,
I joyfully weep,
I return home.

*

I - body of the soul,
I live, I love,
I experience, I learn,
I – vapor, I rise
I joyfully
Return home.

"Cidar," Konna continued, "When you decide that it is time for you to drop your physical body and go to the astral plane, you confront yourselves with the question: is this your last lifetime in the physical plane? If you think, as a spirit, that you still have some issues you need to resolve by returning to the physical plane, think again. The astral plane is a replica of the physical plane, except you do not have a physical body. Thus, you would eventually learn in the astral plane of existence that you would be fully capable of resolving any issue or concern without having to return to the physical plane. In doing so, you would be able to avoid the primordial, the prenatal, and birth pains in addition to the pain of growing up. And you would consequently accelerate your spiritual growth and have the desire to softly and easily move to and be conscious of HER. It all depends on you and you alone. Just remember you are the path-walker," Konna paused for a moment and then asked, "Do you have any question to ask, Cidar?"

Cidar thought for a brief moment and said, "Yes Konna, I would like to ask you about death. What is death?"

Konna with a wide smile on her beautiful face responded, "Death in HER consciousness is thought of as a transformation and liberation. It gives the soul an opportunity to raise its vibration to a higher level of existence and it liberates it from the prison of the physical body. Tagore, an Indian philosopher and poet, said, *"Death is not extinguishing the light; it is only putting out the lamp because the dawn has come."* In the Low-Energy Reality you believe in death because it is the only way out of that reality. In HER, death does not exist because we believe there is no end to who you are."

Death

Is a freeing thought,
A birth of something new,
And,
Cure the fever called life.

Fear it not.

Konna disappeared. Cidar was left enchanted and spellbound.

My Last Lifetime

They told me I have only one lifetime
To reach total enlightenment.
I said you must be fools,
For I would surely lose.
They countered,
How about two, ten, a thousand
I said,
That's more like it.
Thus I embarked upon not one or two,
But hundreds of lifetimes to reach enlightenment.
Now I realize there is no referee,
Or judge or even God to decide for me.
Multiple lifetimes are a game
Of cosmic miscue.
Thus I make this lifetime my last
And most magical one,
For I have so much enlightenment to attain.
Waiting for me in higher planes of light,
So much love to experience
Where love is the only language spoken.

So much to look forward to
When I dance with the light of my soul.

13- The Higher Self Avatar: Aalii

"Nothing is certain but uncertainty."
                Mahdy Khaiyat,
                From "A Cornucopia of Aphorisms"

As Cidar was writing down what Konna revealed to him, he began to doubt what he had learned so far. The early skepticism and doubt that he set aside had surfaced again. What if the whole thing is a lie? What if his higher self's different Avatars are nothing but his own ego personified? But then, his life as a result of this experience has become more joyful and peaceful. After all, they had saved his life during the truck accident and that cannot be denied. With that thought, he fell asleep.

Summer began to wind down. Cidar's two-week vacation would soon end. He had to go back to work the following week. The next day he felt an urge to again go to the tree at Mont Taba to meditate. To his surprise, he found three chairs in the rose garden. Two figures appeared. Cidar sat down on his usual chair. Female and male figures sat on the other two chairs. They appeared to him as the most beautiful people he had seen thus far. They were indeed becoming more and more beautiful in appearance.

"Our names are Aalii and we represent the feminine and the masculine energies used in any creative process. We are your Higher Self and we are going to speak with one thought and one voice," Aalii spoke. Cidar was totally captivated and spellbound by their beauty and could not utter a word.

"We are here to answer any question you may have and to address any concern or doubt you may bring up," Aalii continued. "We are aware of your thought that what we may be telling you is a lie or a misrepresentation of the truth. The three heavenly religions, Judaism, Christianity and Islam, have said that God has created the whole universe and every living organism in it to worship him. However, they fail to explain why God wanted to create this universe and every living thing in it to worship him. In addition, there was never an explanation as to who created God. These three religions had also criticized science, not acknowledging the discoveries of the age of the universe and the planet earth. We, in turn, with our interpretation of creation, wanted to bring religion and science closer to one another. Instead of competing against one another, the two would cooperate to get closer to unveiling the secret of creation."

"When science and spiritual depth travel together,
the distance to the destination is shortened."

Mahdy Khaiyat
From "A Cornucopia of Aphorism"

After a brief pause, Aalii continued, "Cidar, you have already asked the question of who created the universe and why before you reincarnated to your present lifetime. We came to work with you to shed light and give some answers to your questions. You have the liberty to decide whether what we tell you is closer to your truth or not.

"Furthermore, you were wondering whether we are part of your ego," Aalii continued. "We say no. We are not part of your ego. As we mentioned before, the ego is a level of energy which can only exist in the Low-Energy Reality. We are part of you that exists in HER, High-Energy Reality. We have no ego. However, your ego which exists only in the Low-Energy Reality can either be positive or negative. The positive ego is the energy that gives you a little push to go over the hump in your spiritual growth. One example is when you decided to move from the animal kingdom into the human kingdom; your ego gave you the needed energy to get through, and that is positive.

Spiritual Ride

Exhausted on a spinning wheel,
A ride to eternity.

Ego negatively dying,
Ego positively evolving.

Life continuously melting
In a pot of spirituality.

"The negative ego, on the other hand, is the energy that stands in the way of your growth. You were able to tap into it after the big bang when you found yourselves comparing each other, better than and worse than level of energy. The negative ego would always seek to delay your spiritual growth by trying to destroy what you have been able to accomplish. It would continue doing so until you learned how to deal with it and transform it into a positive ego. One way to do so would be by assigning the ego to do a specific task in your consciousness. With close supervision and clear expressed limitation, never allow it to do anything else."

My Ego

A knock on the door of my inner world was heard.
My Ego appeared as I opened the door and left it ajar.

"I have a message from the outer world," he murmured.
I said "Thank you" as I took the sealed envelope.

"May I come in?" he inquired
As I was about to close the door.

I asked for an explanation
For his intrusion.

He replied:
I would like to open the sealed envelope, read the message,
Perhaps even analyze it, and prepare a reply for you.

"No thank you," I answered.
I require no assistance from you.

I have my higher self, my self-love, my self-confidence
And my self-worth as my assistants,

And will give it to you to deliver to my outer world.

"My dear Ego, be the positive energy I would like you to be
And remain my best deliveryman.
Thank you again.

"We hope we are able to put an end to your doubts, Cidar," Aalii continued in unison.

"I believe so," Cidar responded. "There is one thing I would like to ask you, if I may," Cidar said.

"Yes, please go ahead," Aalii responded with kind smiles.

"While visiting the Hindu temple, I heard some people talking about Karma," Cidar proceeded. "Would you please explain what it means?"

"Certainly," Aalii responded. "Karma is a level of energy that could only be experienced in the Low-Energy Reality, more so in the Causal plane of existence where cause and effect take place. When you send out a certain level of energy, the same level of energy will come back to you. In fact, Newton's Third Law of Motion explains this fact in your physical plane:

"When you push on an object with a certain force, the object would push back on you with a force of an equal magnitude and opposite in direction.

"As far as energy is concerned, when you give out positive energy, positive energy will come back to you. Similarly, when you give out negative energy, negative energy will return to you. This process is called Karma in Hinduism. It suggests that when you do a good deed, a good and similar deed would be done to you, and when you do a bad deed, a bad deed would be done to you. If a person kills another, the killer, if she or he believes in Karma, would create another person to kill her or him in order to balance the Karma. In the Physical plane this action might take several lifetimes to manifest.

"However, we would suggest that this should not be the case at all. In case of bad Karma, a person has a choice to work around the guilt associated with doing a bad deed and defuse the effect of bad Karma from happening. If she or he chooses to recognize the fact that there is a bad deed to deal with, acknowledges that she or he has instigated this deed, repents and forgives her or himself for doing it and completely changes and refrains from doing it again. Then and only then, a similar bad deed would not take place. Self-repentance and self-forgiveness would defuse the bad Karma effect.

Hindrance

It is up to us to let our Karma rule
And suffer for our past actions like fools.

The new age movement wishes to control,
Like a religion, with no remorse.

The karmic forces were created
To limit our freedom without being stated.

Now it is up to us to stop the trauma
And move beyond this miserable drama:

It is up to us to recognize that
A hindrance to our growth materializes.

It is up to us to acknowledge the truth that

WE

create this obstacle to our spiritual growth.

It is up to us to forgive our souls
For all the wounds we have caused.

It is up to us to put out the fire inside
And transform to the beings our hearts and souls desire.

It is up to us, it is up to us.

"Thank you, Aalii. Now I see the possibilities of defusing the effect of bad Karma," Cidar acknowledged.

"Cidar," Aalii continued, "during these few months of summer you have fully lived and encountered all aspects of your soul. Your soul has grown before your very eyes. You are the rocks of Mont Taba, the water streams that flow down the mountain. You are the tree you hug and meditate by every day. You are the neighbor's cat. You are the blue jay, you are the spider, you are the ants, you are the pen, and you are Safeer."

'We began as a mineral,
We emerged into plant life
And into animal state,
And then into being human,
And always we have forgotten
Our former state,
Except in early spring,
When we slightly recall
Being green again.'

                    Rumi

Evolution of a Soul

Once I was a rock,
Against all odds, solid and firm I stood.

Then I was water,
Around obstacles I flowed to continue my journey.

When I was a tree, I stood tall and brushed the heavens
Yet my roots were deep into the earth.

When I was a bird, I learned
To fly and freely soar.

Now I am human, I am learning
How to love and be loved.

"How do we know that?" Aalii reflected. "Because
we are you and you are us. For a long time, you and
your conscious level were not aware of us. However, we patiently waited for you to be aware and
unite with us. You and only you have decided to

reach out and touch us, and we in turn, responded to your request. We are deeply delighted by your decision. Now we are celebrating our union, and together we will continue the journey."

Reunion

A wound that almost became a memory
Is healed.
A vacuum of connection that haunted the hearts
Is filled.

Our innocence
Taught us to wait;
What was in the hearts
Remains in the hearts,

A spark of a reminder
Of the love that
Has always been there;
A bond that was never shattered,
Never broken,
Never died.

*

The sun sets with its
Fire of passion;
The moon cools the heavens with its
Silver rays
And
The rite of spring
Blooms with its roses.

Together,
They celebrate
Our reunion.

Aalii paused for a few seconds and continued, "We together have reached the reality we were longing for. You know how to reach us. We will always be near. We sing together, we laugh together, we dance together.

Together

We play music,
No need for instruments.

Together,
We dance to
The beat-less beat.

Together,
We sing
The word-less song.

When both become whole,
When one plus one is one – not two.

For the joy of living;

This is our dance,
This is our music,

This is our song
When our hearts
Beat in unison.

****

Sunny's Song

I am a child of the universe,
Born of the goddess and god
Embodied in soul, with mind
To find what is real, what is love
What is kind.

Ego wanders, controls in vain
A crack in the heart opens wide
Shadow and light clear the sight
With multi-faced grace my guide

singing:

"You make the path you are walking
You choose the yes and the no
We're always here – closer than near
Ask us for help as you go."

The universe spins on the head of a pin
Nothing to lose, nothing to win.

Eleanor Grandfield,
Santa Barbara

Cidar walked home that day with a deep-rooted feeling of belonging to something larger than he had ever imagined. He would never feel alone again. He is a part of a greater whole. He has returned home.

"I come from elsewhere, and though I do not know where that is, I am certain to return there in the end. "When I die, I will soar with angels, and when I die to the angels, what I shall become, you cannot imagine."

Rumi

"So journey my friend to the beloved Allah,
Where you find your eternal home.
Like drops of water seeking to unite
With the vast ocean of bliss".

Omar Al-Khayyam
Translated from Farsi to Arabic
By Ahmed Rami, and from Arabic
To English by Ibrahim Ibn Salma

Coming Home

I - water of the sea,
I - vapor, I rise,
I – clouds above the mountains,
I experience, I learn,
I joyfully weep,
I return home.

*

I - body of the soul,
I live, I love,
I experience, I learn,
I – vapor, I rise
I joyfully
Return home.

The following day Cidar asked Safeer to meet him at Mont Taba near the tree. Even though Safeer already knew the story, Cidar wanted to tell it to him in person. To Cidar's surprise, the blue jay, the neighbor's cat, the spider, the ants, the rock, and the pen also showed up.

Cidar started:

"At the beginning ...."

"Ancora Imparo"

I

  am

    Still

      Learning

Michelangelo

*

"Paradise is not a different world; it is a different way to look at our world."

John Moriarty, Irish philosopher

"Oh, life,
I have borrowed you from light and
to light I shall deliver you."

With Peace & Love
Ibrahim Ibn Salma

Acknowledgments

I am very grateful to Orin and DaBen for their insightful information which helped me imagine this story. I am also grateful to Judy Herrick and Mahdy Khaiyat for their impeccable editing and constructive critiques. I thank the following people for their suggestions and guidance: Eleanor Grandfield, Birgitta Hansson, Edith Lorscheider, Dr. Karl Blasius , and Nancy Keller.

All poems are written by the author except as indicated.

Rumi's poems and quotes are translated by Coleman Barks.

Hafiz's poem, and Meister Eckhart's quote are translated by Daniel Ladinsky.

www.ingramcontent.com/pod-product-compliance
Lightning Source LLC
Chambersburg PA
CBHW021222260626
47172CB00002B/554